THE PUPPY PLACE

NALA

THE PUPPY PLACE

Don't miss any of these other stories by Ellen Miles!

THE PUPPY PLACE

NALA

ELLEN
MILES

SCHOLASTIC INC.

For Miriam

Copyright © 2015 by Ellen Miles
Cover art by Tim O'Brien
Original cover design by Steve Scott

All rights reserved. Published by Scholastic Inc., *Publishers since 1920*. SCHOLASTIC and associated logos are trademarks and/or registered trademarks of Scholastic Inc.

The publisher does not have any control over and does not assume any responsibility for author or third-party websites or their content.

This book is a work of fiction. Names, characters, places, and incidents are either the product of the author's imagination or are used fictitiously, and any resemblance to actual persons, living or dead, business establishments, events, or locales is entirely coincidental.

ISBN 978-0-545-85723-9

10 9 8 7 6   18 19 20

Printed in the U.S.A.   40

First printing 2016

CHAPTER ONE

"Maybe it'll be floor hockey," said Sammy, sweeping a pretend hockey stick to pass a pretend ball to David.

"My cousin plays that at college," David said, sending a pretend pass back to Sammy. "It sounds like a blast."

Charles noticed that neither of his friends bothered to pretend-pass to him. They probably figured he would mess up the shot, pretend or not. Charles Peterson was good at a lot of things — for example, taking care of dogs and understanding their special language and ways — but unlike his friends, he was not a natural

1

athlete. Also unlike them, he could not get himself excited about the "special new activity" Ms. Helm had promised they would be starting that day in PE.

Their gym teacher had been dropping hints about it for weeks, telling the second graders how much fun they were about to have. "Everybody always says this is the best unit of the year," she'd promised. Now, as Charles and his friends walked to school, they tried to guess what it might be.

Charles had asked his older sister, Lizzie, if she remembered what she had done in second-grade PE (she was in fourth grade now), but she didn't. "All I remember is dumb old square dancing last year," she said. "Sweaty hands and everybody crashing into each other."

Lizzie wasn't too much into PE, either. Like Charles, she was mainly interested in dogs. In fact, she was totally dog-crazy. She was the one who had decided that their family should foster puppies.

Their family included Lizzie and Charles's younger brother, Adam (known as the Bean); their dad, a firefighter; and their mom, a newspaper reporter. By now the Petersons had fostered dozens of puppies, taking care of them just long enough to find the perfect home for each one. Charles remembered every single puppy, and he would have loved to keep them all — but that wasn't how fostering worked. Sometimes he still had dreams about Moose, the huge but cowardly Great Dane they'd had for a while, or Lucy the long-eared hound mix. He knew they had both gone to terrific homes, but he wished he could still play with them now and then.

"Wouldn't that be great, Cheese?" Sammy said, elbowing Charles in the ribs.

"Wouldn't what be great?" Charles stared at his friend. He'd been lost in thought about puppies and had not been paying attention to the conversation.

"Learning circus stuff, like how to swing on a trapeze or walk a tightrope or be a clown, like David's cousin. I heard they do that at some schools."

Charles shrugged. "I guess," he said. He pictured himself trying to balance as he tiptoed along a tightrope strung high above the playground. His stomach lurched. *Hmm*, he thought. Maybe it wouldn't be so great after all. He'd really rather be in his own backyard, tossing a soft rubber football for Buddy, the one foster puppy the Petersons had not been able to give up. Now the sweet little brown pup was part of their family, and Charles never got tired of hanging out with him.

Charles looked at Sammy and David. They were both good friends, but his *best* friend was definitely Buddy. Who else could he tell all his secrets to? Who else was always, always happy to see him and ready to do anything Charles wanted to do? Which, Charles realized, definitely did not include walking on tightropes.

"What would you want PE to be?" Sammy asked. "I mean, if you could pick anything."

Charles shrugged again. "Probably something I could do with Buddy," he said. "Like when we did agility. That was the most fun." He and Lizzie had taken agility classes with Buddy and one of their foster puppies, a sheltie named Gizmo. Charles remembered that Gizmo had not caught on very quickly, but Buddy had been a natural at running the special obstacle course.

"I don't think they're going to be doing dog sports at school anytime soon," said David.

"Nope," agreed Sammy. "But I bet Ms. Helm has something awesome planned for us, whatever it is."

David nodded eagerly, but Charles was still lost in picturing Buddy running through the yellow tunnel at agility class, his short little tail wagging as he disappeared into its mouth. When he popped out, he'd scramble toward the seesaw to run up one side, balance in the middle, then run down the other end, making the seesaw come down with a bang as he sprang off it. Buddy always grinned as he did the obstacles. He was obviously having the time of his life.

A school bus passed the boys, and Sammy waved at the kids looking out the back window. One of them made a funny face, and Sammy made one back, sticking out his tongue as far as it would go.

The bus trundled on down the block, passing Mr. Mike, the crossing guard. He waved and made a face, too. "Look at Mr. Mike, cracking himself up again," said Sammy, laughing and waving. Mr. Mike was always in a good mood, even on gloomy or freezing cold days. He was always ready for a high five or Charles's latest knock-knock joke. He'd been king of that corner for as long as Charles could remember, and he made it fun to arrive at school every day.

By now, the friends were just a block away from school, passing the little brick house that was always super decorated for the holidays: huge skeletons dancing all over the lawn at Halloween; a sled and reindeer, all lit up, on the roof for Christmas; a tree full of colorful eggs at Easter.

At the moment, the house looked pretty plain except for some cutout snowflakes in the window and a snowman banner waving from the front porch — even though they hadn't had any real snowstorms so far.

"Hey, what's that?" Sammy pointed to a quick flash of orangey red disappearing behind the garage. "Was it a fox?"

"A cat?" guessed David.

Charles had only caught a glimpse, but he shook his head. "No," he said. "I'm pretty sure it was a puppy."

CHAPTER TWO

Sammy darted forward to look around the other side of the garage. "There it is!" he yelled.

"Not so loud, you'll scare it," called Charles. He scanned what he could see of the brick house's backyard, watching for another flash of color against the gray and brown tree trunks.

Nothing.

"Where is it?" Charles asked. "Where'd it go?"

"It disappeared again. It's fast. Maybe it *is* a fox," Sammy said, walking back to join them.

"What if it's a fox with rabies?" David asked. "I've heard of that. They can bite people and make them really sick."

Charles shook his head. "I don't think it's a fox. Foxes are smaller and lower to the ground. They have black face masks and tiny little feet, almost like cat feet." He had watched a fox trotting across a field one time, up in the country where his cousins lived. He'd never forgotten it. It was one of the coolest, prettiest things he'd ever seen.

He peered again into the backyard, wishing he could poke around in there, but he knew it wasn't polite to walk into other people's yards. Anyway, there wasn't much time before the bell rang and school started for the day. Mr. Mason was a really nice teacher, but he did not like it when people were late to class. He didn't like it at all.

"There! What's that!" David pointed as something red flashed around the far side of the house, heading straight toward the corner where Mr. Mike stood.

"I see it!" Sammy threw down his bookbag and took off running.

"Don't chase it!" Charles yelled. Now that he had a better view of the animal, he was sure that it was a puppy — a beautiful, small-boned girl puppy, almost as pretty as that fox he'd seen. She had a long, feathery tail and a long, pointed nose. Her rusty-red fur was ablaze against the gray background, and she had a thick white ruff around her neck and an apron of pure white fur on her chest. She was thin, though, and Charles could tell by the way she ran, with her ears back and her tail held low, that she was afraid. Charles looked for a collar or a trailing leash, but he couldn't see either one.

"Grab her, Mr. Mike!" yelled Sammy.

"No!" yelled Charles. He was just about positive that if someone tried to grab that frightened puppy, she would veer away and run as fast as she could in the opposite direction — maybe into the street.

But it was too late. Mr. Mike heard Sammy, and he turned around in time to see the dog charging toward him. He squatted down and opened his arms wide. "Here, pup!" he called. "Come to Mr. Mike!"

Charles was right. The puppy dashed to Mr. Mike's left and darted into the street, with Sammy following close behind. "No!" yelled Charles. He threw down his own bookbag and took off running up the sidewalk, with David right behind him. They both stayed on their side of the street, but Sammy dashed across, following the puppy.

Screeech! Charles heard the sound of squealing brakes as one of the drivers on the busy street came to a quick stop.

"Hey, kid!" yelled the driver. "What do you think you're doing?" He shook a fist at Sammy, who had chased the puppy all the way to the other side of the street. Then he turned and frowned at Mr. Mike, giving him a "what's-up-with-that?" gesture, his hands held up in surprise. Finally, he drove off down the road, shaking his head.

Mr. Mike was not smiling now. His face was white, and his mouth was a thin line. He pointed across the street at Sammy. "You stay right where you are, young man," he shouted. "Do not move a muscle. You hear me?"

Sammy nodded, looking down at his shoes.

By then, David and Charles had arrived at Mr. Mike's corner. He glared down at them. "Are you two going to pull any hijinks like that today? Because I can tell you, I've had just about enough for one morning."

"No, sir," said David.

"We won't," said Charles. "And Sammy didn't mean to mess up. He just wanted to catch that puppy. I think she's a stray."

Mr. Mike was still frowning. "That may be so, but you're all old enough to know better than to run into a busy street. Aren't you?" He didn't wait for an answer. Instead, he picked up his red STOP sign, looked up and down the road, and stepped off the curb, holding the sign high to signal any approaching drivers. "Now get a move on," he said, "or you'll be late for school."

He walked partway across the road with them and stopped in the middle, still holding up the sign.

"Will you keep an eye out for that puppy?" Charles dared to ask. He had never seen Mr. Mike in a bad mood before.

Mr. Mike rolled his eyes. "Your friend could have gotten hit by a car, and you're still worrying about that scrawny stray?" But then his face softened. "Poor little thing," he said, shaking his head. "She looked pretty scared."

"So, will you?" asked Charles.

Mr. Mike nodded. "Okay," he said. "But you boys have to promise me: no more running into the street. Not ever. Not for a puppy, not for a ball, not for Santa Claus with a bag full of toys."

Charles and David nodded.

"And you tell your friend Sammy what I said, too," said Mr. Mike.

They nodded again. One of the waiting cars beeped a polite little beep, letting them know that they were holding up traffic.

Finally, Mr. Mike smiled at them. "I'm just glad you're all okay," he said. "Now skedaddle, will you?" He waved them the rest of the way across the street, then went back to his corner.

As Charles and David joined Sammy, Charles

heard the school bell ring. "We'd better get moving," he said. "We won't be late if we run."

Sammy shook his head. "Guess we're going to be late," he said, pointing across the street. Their bookbags lay in a heap where they'd tossed them on the sidewalk in front of the brick house.

CHAPTER THREE

Mr. Mason definitely did not look happy when Charles, Sammy, and David arrived, panting, in his classroom. He stood with his arms folded across his chest, frowning as he watched them come in.

"Sorry!" said Charles. "There was this dog, and —"

Mr. Mason held up a hand and shook his head. "Don't tell me about it. Not right now. You need to get yourselves to Ms. Guzman's office."

Charles gulped. "The principal?"

"She wants to speak to all three of you. She is

not pleased about what happened out there this morning."

David, Sammy, and Charles looked at one another. Mr. Mike must have already radioed in a report. Charles noticed David's face flushing pink. "First time?" he whispered to his friend as they headed out of room 2B and down the hall. David nodded. "Me, too," said Charles. He had never been sent to see the principal before. In fact, he'd barely ever been in any kind of trouble at school. He felt a knot in his belly. "I wonder if she'll call our parents."

"She probably already did," said Sammy as they entered the school office, at the end of the hall. "Sometimes they're even here waiting for you."

He sounded like an old pro. "How many times have you been here?" David asked after they'd given their names to Mrs. Serota, the school secretary.

Sammy settled himself comfortably on one of the red plastic chairs outside Ms. Guzman's door. "I can't remember," he said. "Three? Four? Maybe six?"

David gasped, and Charles noticed that his face turned as pale as that puppy's white ruff. "But it's probably not so bad, right?" David asked. "I mean, Ms. Guzman seems really nice when she's out in the hall saying hello to everybody in the morning."

Charles nodded in agreement. "She knows everybody's name, and she even notices if you have a cool bookbag or a new haircut or something." He could picture short, stocky Ms. Guzman smiling and nodding and high-fiving kids as they streamed past her into the school's lobby.

"That's an act," whispered Sammy. "She's really mean when you're alone in there with her." He held his hands up like claws and gave a scary growl. "Like a grizzly bear, man. She —"

The door opened.

"Come in, boys," said Ms. Guzman. She held the door for them as they filed into her office. Charles felt her hand on his head, a light and gentle touch, as he went by.

"Sit, please," she said. The boys perched on chairs in front of Ms. Guzman's big desk as she circled around to take her own seat behind it. She set her elbows on the desk, leaned forward, and looked at each of the boys in turn. "So," she said, very calmly, "I hear we had an exciting morning."

Charles looked at Sammy. Obviously, Ms. Guzman was not a grizzly bear.

Sammy gave him a little grin and a shrug as if to say, *I was just kidding.*

"Is there something funny about it, Sammy?"

asked Ms. Guzman. "If there is, please share the joke."

Sammy bit his lip. "No," he said, shaking his head. "I messed up. I know I did."

Ms. Guzman nodded. "Good. I'm glad to hear you understand the seriousness of what happened. Mr. Mike was very upset. If you'd been hurt, he would have felt like it was his fault."

Sammy looked down at his hands. "I'll tell him I'm sorry," he said.

"Good," said Ms. Guzman. "I was going to suggest that an apology was in order. What else?"

"No running into the street?" David asked.

Ms. Guzman smiled. "Absolutely no running into the street."

"And don't leave your bookbag somewhere so you have to go back and get it and then be late to class," Charles added.

"I see that you boys have it all figured out

already." Ms. Guzman leaned back in her seat. "Terrific. All I expect is that you focus on getting to school on time, in one piece. I expect you to do your best. That might not mean you are perfect, but as long as you're trying, that's what matters. Do you understand?" She pointed to a poster on her wall. It showed a picture of a muscle-y guy in red shorts climbing up a high, steep cliff. The caption said ALWAYS DO YOUR BEST.

Charles could tell by now that Ms. Guzman was not really going to punish them. "Yes," he and his friends chorused. He slumped back in his seat and let out a breath. Of course he would try to Do His Best. Not that he would climb a cliff like that — not in a million years. That guy in the shorts was out of his mind!

Ms. Guzman nodded. "Okay, boys. You may return to class."

Charles pulled his gaze away from the climber

in the poster and looked at Ms. Guzman. "What about the dog?" he asked.

"What dog?" asked Ms. Guzman.

"The puppy I was chasing," said Sammy. "Didn't you hear about that?"

"Of course," said Ms. Guzman. "I forgot for a moment. Well, hopefully the puppy has found her way home by now, where she belongs. Just as the three of you belong in room 2B." She stood up and checked her watch. "Actually, your class is probably on their way to the gym right now. You can meet them there." She went to her door and opened it for them.

"Phew," said David as they walked down the hall to the gym. "That wasn't so bad."

"She was nice — this time," said Sammy. "But you should see her when she really gets going. It's like her teeth turn into fangs, and she starts to snarl, and . . ."

Charles just shook his head at his friend. "Yeah, right," he said. "And Mr. Mason is a vampire in his spare time."

"Maybe he is!" said Sammy. "Maybe if we spied on him, we'd see him slipping out of the house at night, wearing a black cape, and —"

Charles stopped listening. Sammy could be so silly sometimes. Right then, Charles just wanted to enjoy the sweet feeling of relief. He had been sent to the principal's office — and he had survived! The knot in his stomach was gone. Except . . . he pictured that poor little puppy, running scared and alone through the streets, and the knot came right back. Somehow, Charles knew that the puppy needed his help.

CHAPTER FOUR

As the three boys approached the gym doors, Charles spotted his class coming down the hall, led by Mr. Mason. For once, everybody was in line and quiet, the way they were supposed to be when they were in the halls. But then Nicky saw Charles and his friends and yelled out, "Hey, what happened? Did you get suspended?"

Somebody hooted, and someone else sang out, "You're in trouble now!"

Mr. Mason stopped and turned to the class, crossing his arms. Charles couldn't see his face, but he could imagine his teacher's expression as he waited for everyone to quiet down again.

"That's better," Mr. Mason said when they were silent. He took a few more steps toward the gym doors, opened them, and waved his class inside. As Charles and his friends passed, he raised his eyebrows. "Everything okay?" he asked.

Charles nodded.

"Good," said Mr. Mason. "Have fun in PE."

Charles looked around as he walked into the gym with the rest of his class. He didn't see any trapezes swinging from the rafters or goals set up for floor hockey. The only new item in the room was a big poster, pinned up on the wall beneath a basketball hoop. As Charles got closer, he could read the headline across the top: WELCOME TO THE FITNESS CLUB. The colorful chart had lines down one side for names, and columns of activities across the top.

"Welcome, class 2B!" Ms. Helm grinned as she clapped her hands for attention. "We're going to have a blast over the next few weeks," she said. "Has everybody heard about the President's Challenge?"

Charles groaned. Sure, he had. He'd heard all about it from Harry, an older boy who had become his friend when the Petersons were fostering Princess, a spoiled little Yorkshire terrier. Harry had loved the President's Challenge. "It was great," he'd told Charles. "I learned so much about myself and what I could do." Charles guessed that he would probably not like it as much as Harry had. After all, Harry was a super athlete who was a star on the high school basketball *and* baseball teams.

Most of the kids in their class raised their hands. "Can anyone tell us about it?" asked Ms. Helm. "Nicky?"

"It's to see how strong you are," said Nicky, flexing his arm muscles, "and how fast you can run."

Ms. Helm nodded. "That's certainly part of it. Mainly, it's about fitness. We'll be testing you all on the President's Challenge for real when you're in fourth grade. This year, we're just going to be learning about it and practicing for it. We'll learn why fitness is important. We'll also learn how fit we are right now, and we'll learn how to work on our fitness."

"Ms. Helm?" Lucy raised her hand. "What is fitness, exactly?"

Ms. Helm beamed. "Excellent question. Let's talk about how our bodies work." She went to the far corner of the gym and pulled out a whiteboard on wheels.

Charles settled in to listen as Ms. Helm started to talk about muscles and lungs and nutrition. Maybe this wasn't going to be so bad after all. As long as he didn't have to do stuff in front of everybody else and make a fool of himself, everything would be fine.

Ms. Helm covered the whiteboard with diagrams and words, then finally looked up to check the clock. "We have time to try one activity," she said. "Let's see, how about . . . push-ups?" She rubbed her hands together, smiling as if push-ups were the most exciting activity in the world.

Charles did not like push-ups. He'd tried them before and he just couldn't do them very well. His front would sag down when he tried to lift it off the ground, his shoulders would get tired, and his wrists would hurt.

"Pair up, everyone," said Ms. Helm. "We'll help our partners by counting how many push-ups they do while I time the group." She held up the purple stopwatch that hung on a bright pink cord around her neck. "You'll have three minutes to do as many push-ups as you can." She explained a little bit about proper form and then gave a demonstration, dropping down on the squishy blue plastic mat that covered part of the gym floor. She jumped to her feet and blew her whistle for attention as she held up the stopwatch again. "Get ready," she said, "get set, *go!*"

Charles trudged up the front steps at home after school that day, feeling discouraged. He had been able to do only two — well, two and a half — push-ups. It was embarrassing to fill in the little box next to his name on the chart and see that even skinny little Beth D. had done five. He was not looking forward to the next few weeks of PE; that was for sure.

Worse, even though he had kept his eyes peeled the whole way home, he had not caught one glimpse of the pretty little puppy from the morning. Had she found her way home? Charles hoped so, but he worried that she was still out there somewhere, lost or hurt and probably hungry and afraid. He pushed open the door, feeling tired and sad.

"Charles Peterson," said his mother. She stood in the front hall, as if she'd been waiting for him.

Charles winced. "What?" he asked.

"You know what," said his mom. "Ms. Guzman called me this afternoon, and I was not happy to hear what she had to say."

"But Sammy's the one who —" Charles began, but he could tell by his mother's face that it was hopeless.

"Just promise me you'll get yourself to school on time tomorrow morning, no matter what," said his mom. "Otherwise, I'll have to start walking with you."

Charles shuddered. Who wanted their mom walking them to school, unless maybe you were a kindergartner? "I promise," he said. "But if I see that puppy —"

"I don't care if you see a dragon," said his mom. "You get yourself to school before that bell rings."

Charles nodded. "Okay," he said.

But the next morning, before he left the house, he slipped a couple of slices of ham out of the package in the fridge, stuck them into a plastic bag, and put it in his pocket. It never hurt to have tempting treats with you if you were trying to catch a dog.

As he and Sammy and David walked to school, they looked down every cross street and peeked into backyards, but they did not see the dog anywhere.

"I hope she's okay," said David as they neared Mr. Mike's corner.

"I bet she is," said Sammy.

Charles wasn't so sure, but he hoped Sammy was right.

Mr. Mike gave them each a smile and a high five. At least he wasn't still mad at them. "Have you seen that puppy?" Charles asked him.

Mr. Mike shook his head. "No, and to be honest, I hope I never do. I hope she's home, safe and sound. I don't like to see dogs *or* kids in the street."

As the day went on, Charles tried to forget about the dog. He did his best to concentrate on a spelling quiz, some practice with fractions, and his report on Peru. Still, he couldn't seem to get that puppy's pretty red coat and fluffy white ruff out of his head. He wanted to see her again and know for sure that she was okay.

At the end of the day, Mr. Mason gave them time to work on book reports that were due the next day. Charles's was on a book by Beverly Cleary called *Ralph S. Mouse*, and he was almost done. He dawdled at his desk, wondering if he should draw a picture of Ralph for the cover, then got up to sharpen his pencil.

He gazed out the window as he used the pencil sharpener, thinking again about the runaway puppy. Then his eye caught a motion behind the green dumpster that sat next to the school's maintenance shed.

A blur of coppery fur, the twitch of a fluffy white-tipped tail.

Charles threw down his pencil. He ran out of the classroom, ignoring Mr. Mason's surprised yell, dashed down the hall, and charged right out the school's back door. Somehow, he remembered to close it quietly behind him so he wouldn't scare the puppy. He stepped outside, looking to the right and left, breathing hard. He tiptoed toward the dumpster, feeling in his pocket for the baggie full of ham. *"Pssst,"* he said, making the little noise that always caught Buddy's attention. "Here, little pup," he called.

But when he got to the other side of the dumpster, all he saw was a banana peel and a wad of paper towels.

Charles sighed. He picked up the trash and threw it into the dumpster, then glanced around again. No puppy.

The back door slammed open. "Mr. Peterson," he heard someone say in a very stern voice.

He stepped out from behind the dumpster and gulped when he saw Ms. Guzman standing in the doorway with her hands on her hips.

"Would you please join me in my office?" she asked before turning on her heel and striding back inside.

CHAPTER FIVE

Charles slumped in his seat, staring at the floor. Here he was, in the principal's office for the second time in two days. How could that be? He wasn't a bad kid, really he wasn't.

So far Ms. Guzman had not said a word. He'd followed her down the hall into her office. She had shown him to his seat and taken her own. Then she removed her glasses and rubbed her eyes. Charles thought he heard her sigh. As he waited for her to say something, he looked up at the ALWAYS DO YOUR BEST poster and winced. He was pretty certain he had not just Done His Best to stay out of trouble.

"I'm not sure what's happening here, Charles," the principal finally said as she put her glasses back on and looked up at him. "You've never misbehaved this way before. Can you explain why you seem to have moved into my office?"

"It's all because of the puppy," Charles said. "I saw her! I saw her out the window, and I couldn't stand to lose her again."

Ms. Guzman waited.

Charles hung his head. "I know it was wrong to leave my classroom," he said.

"Not to mention the school building," Ms. Guzman added.

"Not to mention the school building," Charles echoed. "But — I didn't run into any streets!" He managed a hopeful grin, but Ms. Guzman did not return it.

"Not running into streets is the very least I expect of you — of all my students," said Ms.

Guzman. "That's not exactly a huge point in your favor." She reached for the phone and pressed an intercom button. "Mrs. Serota, can you get one of Charles Peterson's parents on the phone?"

Charles sank deeper into his seat, groaning. Did she really have to make such a big deal out of it?

"You may wait outside the office," Ms. Guzman told him. "We'll talk some more when your mom or dad arrives."

Charles slunk out the door and plopped down onto one of the red chairs outside Ms. Guzman's office. He folded his arms and stared at the floor. Despite everything that had happened, he couldn't get the image of the puppy out of his mind. This time, he'd seen her a little closer up. Her fur was matted and tangled, and she'd looked like a frightened wild animal as she nosed around the dumpster. Even with her thick coat, he could tell that she was thin and underfed. There was no question in his mind anymore: the puppy was a stray. He drew in a breath and stuck out his chest. The dog needed him, and he would do anything to help her, even if it meant getting into trouble.

"Hey, sport."

Charles looked up to see his dad striding toward him. "Hi, Dad," he said in a tiny voice.

Dad knelt down by Charles's chair. "What's going on?"

"That puppy I told you about at dinner last night? I saw her again!" Charles said.

Dad nodded. "So she's still on the loose. Poor thing."

"That's what I thought!" said Charles eagerly. Dad understood. He cared about puppies, too. "I knew I had to catch her and help her."

"And so you walked out of your classroom, and out of the school building, without asking an adult for permission?" Dad asked. "Maybe I'm not getting the facts right, but that's what Ms. Guzman told me on the phone."

Charles let out a breath. "Yeah," he said. "I guess I did."

Dad frowned and shook his head. Then he put out a hand and helped Charles to his feet. "Let's go talk to the principal about it. I'm on duty, so if I get beeped, I may have to run." He patted the pager on his belt. "Mom was in the middle of writing an article, so I came down."

Ms. Guzman smiled at Dad when they walked in. That made Charles feel a little better. "Thanks for coming, Mr. Peterson," she said as she motioned for them to sit down. "I'm guessing that by now Charles has had some time to think about his behavior and can tell us how he'll be changing his actions in the future."

Charles nodded. "I'm sorry," he said. "I won't do it again."

Ms. Guzman raised her eyebrows. "Won't do what?" she asked.

"I won't leave class without asking," said Charles, "or the school."

"Even for a puppy?" Ms. Guzman asked, raising her eyebrows. She softened a little. "Your dad explained on the phone about how your family fosters puppies. He told me how caring and responsible you are. I get that dogs are really important to you."

Charles nodded.

"But what's *most* important right now is your safety and your education," the principal went on. "Those are our number one priorities. Do we understand each other?"

Charles nodded again. And then again as he promised to Do His Best.

"I think you'd better take him home," Ms. Guzman said to Dad.

Charles gulped. "Am I — am I suspended?" That was one of the worst things that could happen to you at school.

Ms. Guzman laughed and shook her head. "No, you can come right back to school — on time! — tomorrow. But it's almost the end of the day, so I think it's best if you leave with your dad. He may have some more things to say to you on the way home." She picked up some papers and began to shuffle through them.

Dad stood up. "Thank you, Ms. Guzman." He gave Charles a prompting look.

"Thank you, Ms. Guzman," said Charles.

She nodded. "And thank *you* both. I happen to be a pretty huge dog lover myself, and I can't stand to think of puppies in need of homes. I appreciate the work your family does." She cleared her throat and looked down at her papers.

It was time to go. As they left the school, Charles saw his dad's red pickup and headed for it. "Maybe we could drive around a little bit and see if we can find the puppy?" he asked as they both climbed in.

"Your mother is waiting at home," Dad said. "She's not happy about this and neither am I."

"Please, Dad?" Charles begged. "This puppy looks really skinny and scared. She needs us!"

Dad was quiet for a moment. Then he let out a sigh. "Okay. Now you've got me worried about that dog, too. We'll look for a few minutes, then we'll go home."

They cruised up one street and down another, rolling along very slowly as they peered into back-yards. Charles appreciated that his dad did not continue the lecture Ms. Guzman had started. "I guess she's gone," Charles said after a while.

Then, just as his dad turned one last corner, Charles spotted a flash of red against a white picket fence. "There she is!" He was already unbuckling his seat belt as Dad pulled the pickup over to the side of the road.

"Hold on there, buckaroo," Dad said, putting out a hand. "Let's make a plan. Let's make sure we can catch this puppy."

CHAPTER SIX

Charles and Dad sat in the truck and studied the situation. The puppy stood in a short driveway that belonged to a yellow house. She sniffed at the bottom of the wire fence that ran along one side of the driveway. She was so focused on what she was smelling that she had not even looked up when the truck approached. Charles saw a scruffy black dog on the other side of the fence. So at least he knew she wasn't afraid of, or mean to, other dogs. That was good. That meant she'd probably get along with Buddy — if they caught her and brought her home.

"I don't think you should be the one to catch her," Dad said, tapping on the steering wheel. "What if she's a biter?"

Charles shook his head. "She's just a puppy. She won't bite."

"You never know," said Dad. "Look, we don't have long here. She's obviously interested in the dog on the other side of that fence, so we might be able to sneak up on her. And if I pull the truck up to block the end of the driveway" — he eased the truck forward — "she won't really have anywhere to go. That hedge on the other side will block her."

Charles had to admit that his dad was good at making a plan. He nodded and reached into his pocket for some of the ham he'd brought. "Here," he said, handing it to Dad. "I bet she won't be able to resist this."

They opened the truck doors as quietly as they could and slipped out. Charles stood near the truck, watching as Dad snuck closer to the puppy.

She must have smelled or heard him, because all of a sudden she whirled around and stood with her legs straight and her tail held high. Her ears were on alert. She didn't growl. She just watched, her bright eyes focused on Dad, as he inched closer, holding out his hand so she could see the treats he held. She sniffed the air.

What's this? What's this?

When he got too close, she took a few steps backward, looking around as if to find an escape route. The garage blocked her path, so again, she stood still.

Dad tossed a hunk of ham so that it landed right between her delicate front paws. Charles noticed that both front paws were white, like a continuation of her white apron of fur. She looked at the ham, sniffed it, then gobbled it up so fast Charles hardly saw her head move. Then she glanced up at Dad with a hopeful expression.

"Want more?" Dad asked. "You must be hungry if you've been away from home for a while." His voice was low and calm. He tossed another piece. This one landed a little farther from the puppy and a little closer to Charles's dad.

The puppy stared at it. She shook herself all over and sat down. She stood up again. She took one step toward the treat. Then she took two steps back. She stared at the food some more.

Charles could hardly stand it. How long was this going to take? He was dying to hold the beautiful, fluffy pup on his lap, to pet her and whisper calming words to her until she learned she could trust him.

Dad was patient. He tossed another piece, and another. All of them landed between him and the puppy. Finally, she darted forward and snatched one up, then another, and another. While she was on the move, gulping down the food, Dad threw a couple more pieces, even closer to himself. Charles saw his father bend his knees slightly and widen his stance, and knew he was about to make a move.

Charles bent down, too, ready to catch the dog if she tried to run under the truck.

"Okay, puppy, here I come," murmured Dad as he took one quick step toward the dog, arms spread wide.

The puppy dashed around him and charged in Charles's direction, toward the street and freedom. Quickly, Charles sidestepped and cut off her escape, chasing her back toward Dad.

It was like a wild game of tag — with two people as It. The puppy squirted out of Dad's reach and fled back toward Charles. He waved his arms and she veered off toward the open passenger door of the truck. Leaping like a tiny deer, she flew up into Charles's seat.

"Close the other door!" Charles yelled just as he heard the driver's-side door slam shut. He looked through the truck windows to see Mr. Mike grinning on the other side, giving him a thumbs-up.

"Got her!" he said as Charles ran to shut the door she'd jumped through.

"Wow, you showed up just in time," said Dad. He walked around the truck to shake hands with Mr. Mike. "Nice job."

"I was on my way to cover my corner," said Mr. Mike, "but I looked down the street here and saw what was going on. I figured I could help." He grinned at Charles, and they shook hands, too.

Then he picked up the crossing sign he'd tossed to the ground, and gave them a little salute. "Better keep moving," he said. "School's just about to let out."

Charles and Dad opened the truck doors very carefully so the puppy wouldn't escape, and they slowly climbed inside. The puppy sat in the middle of the front seat, staring out the window as if pretending they weren't there. When Charles got close enough, he could feel that she was trembling. She panted nervously, even though it wasn't hot in the pickup. "It's okay," he said softly. "We're not going to hurt you. We're going to take good care of you." He held out his hand for her to sniff. After a moment, she put her nose to his fingers.

I like that smell. Do you have any more of those treats?

Charles slipped a hand into his pocket and found one last piece of ham. He gave it to her and she ate it hungrily. He stroked her gently, feeling how soft her fur was despite the knots and mats in her coat.

Dad started the truck and drove straight home. "I'll go inside and get one of our spare collars and a leash," he said as he pulled into the driveway. "Then maybe you can take her out in the back-yard, and we can have her meet Buddy."

Charles waited in the parked truck, petting the dog. She had stopped trembling, but she was still panting. "You look like a young lioness with that fluffy ruff," he told her. "I think your name should be Nala."

For the first time, she gazed up at him, blinking her shiny coal-black eyes. She held up a paw.

"Wow, maybe that really is your name," said Charles. He wondered if some family was missing this puppy right now. He knew he would be wild if Buddy ran away and was gone for days. Gently, he took her paw and shook it. "Well, it's very nice to meet you, Nala," he said. "I hope you know you've found some friends."

CHAPTER SEVEN

Charles petted Nala gently while he waited for Dad to come back out with a collar and leash. Finally, she seemed to really relax, leaning against him with her eyes partly closed as he scratched her chest and between her soft, fuzzy ears.

She tensed up again when there was a knock at the car window. So did Charles when he saw who was knocking: Mom, looking mad. "Charles," she said when he opened the door to take the collar and leash she handed him.

"I know, I know," he said. He'd almost forgotten about leaving school — but now it all came back in a rush. "I messed up. But look! We caught the puppy. Isn't she pretty?" Nala was trembling again, but Charles touched her softly and she relaxed a bit.

Mom nodded, but she was still frowning. "You'll have plenty of time to take care of her, because you're grounded. Understand? You're not going anywhere except to school for at least a week. Dad and I just talked about it."

Charles made himself busy putting the spare collar on Nala. It was too small at first, but he adjusted it to fit around her thick ruff. "I understand," he said. He knew it was a punishment, but he didn't really mind. He wanted to spend all his time with the sweet, shy puppy.

"I'm disappointed in you, Charles," said Mom. "But I know how much you care about puppies, and I know you want to help this one. We can foster her for a while — as long as you manage to behave yourself. If you end up in Ms. Guzman's office again, we'll have to find another place for the puppy."

Charles clipped the leash onto Nala's collar. "I'll behave," he said. "I promise." He stepped out of the truck and clucked his tongue, encouraging the puppy to come with him. She hung back, frightened. Charles reached in and carefully helped her out. "I'll take her into the backyard," he told his mom. "Buddy can meet her there, and the Bean and Lizzie, too. She needs time to get used to this new place and all the new people."

When he let Nala loose in the fenced backyard, she didn't run around sniffing bushes and checking everything out the way most of their foster puppies did. She just seemed to want to be near him. He walked her around the yard, showing her where she could pee and pointing out the spots where it was okay to dig a little. He picked up Buddy's toy football and tossed it, wondering if she would fetch, but she stuck close by him, almost leaning against his legs.

I feel safe near you, safe for the first time in so long.

When Lizzie got home from her afternoon job (she and some friends had a dog-walking business), she brought Buddy out to meet the new puppy. At first Nala jumped into Charles's lap, but when Buddy play-bowed to her with his tail wagging and a happy grin on his face, she jumped down to say hello. Once she and Buddy had sniffed each other and decided to be friends, Lizzie reached out a hand for Nala to smell. "Hi there, pretty girl," she said in a soft voice.

"I'm calling her Nala," said Charles.

"Good name for a collie, with that gorgeous mane-like ruff," said Lizzie as she gently scratched the top of Nala's head. Nala seemed to understand that Lizzie was another person she could trust. Instead of running back to Charles, she let Lizzie pet her.

Charles wasn't surprised that his sister knew what breed the puppy was; she was good at that. Now that she said it, he knew she was right. Nala looked just like Lassie, the collie from old-time TV.

"This girl's coat needs some care," said Lizzie. "I'll go get a brush and comb. You'll have to tease out some of those knots."

"No problem," said Charles. "Maybe we can give her a bath once that's done."

"We'll see," said Lizzie. "While you're brushing her, I'm going to make some calls. We need to check with the police, and all the shelters and rescue places. We'll have to make sure she doesn't have a microchip, either. What if someone's looking for her?"

Charles did not like to think about giving Nala up. He was already in love with her, and she trusted him. Of course, if she had a real home and family, she belonged with them. He knew Lizzie was right about checking the shelters. And if Nala had a tiny microchip inserted under her skin, there was a special device that could find it and read its information about her owners. But as he worked on her tangles with the brush Lizzie had brought him, he could not help hoping that she was truly a stray, a lost puppy who needed his help.

By the time Lizzie returned, Charles had made his way through most of the worst knots in Nala's coat. He was amazed at how she seemed to trust him; he knew it must have hurt sometimes even though he was as gentle and careful as he could be. "Any news?" he asked, but he didn't even have to wait for his sister's answer. One look at her face told him that she had not learned anything about Nala's home.

She shook her head. "Nobody's looking for a dog. She must have traveled a long way — or else she was abandoned. I told Ms. Dobbins about how shy and scared she is, and . . ."

"What?" Charles asked. He didn't like the way Lizzie was frowning. Ms. Dobbins was the director of Caring Paws, the animal shelter where Lizzie often volunteered. She knew a lot about dogs.

"She thought maybe Nala could have been abused. Maybe she ran away from somebody who was mean to her."

Charles felt tears spring into his eyes. How could anybody be mean to this beautiful, sweet girl? He threw his arms around Nala and held her tight.

"I know," said Lizzie quietly. "It's awful. But maybe we can find her a home where she'll be loved the way she deserves."

Charles sniffed and nodded — though he could hardly stand to think of giving Nala up, even to a loving family.

"Good job on the grooming!" said Lizzie, obviously trying to change the subject. "She looks much, much better." She held out a hand for Nala to sniff. Nala did not shrink back, but she did not leave Charles's lap, either. "She's attached to you already," Lizzie said. "You really do have a way with dogs, especially shy ones."

Charles felt himself blushing. That meant a lot coming from Lizzie. "I wish I had a way with push-ups," he muttered.

Lizzie stared at him. "What?"

"We're doing that yucky fitness testing thing in PE," he said.

"Oooohhh." Lizzie gave him a sympathetic look. "I didn't like that, either. Although I have to say I was pretty good at the stretching part." She sat down next to Charles, stuck her legs out straight, and leaned over them until her fingers almost touched her toes. "I can show you how to do it so you'll get a good score."

By dinnertime that night, Charles was feeling much happier. He had already taught Nala how to sit and shake and play "which hand is the treat in?" She seemed to forget about being shy when she was busy learning and doing. Nala had also behaved perfectly when the Bean petted her gently the way Charles told him to, and she curled up under Charles's chair while he ate dinner. Plus, with Lizzie's coaching, Charles would be ready to tackle the next round of fitness testing. Next time, he would be able to feel proud of the score he filled in next to his name.

CHAPTER EIGHT

Of course, it did not work out the way Charles had pictured it. When his class arrived in the gym the next morning, Ms. Helm announced that they were going to learn the right way to do curl-ups.

She made it sound like a huge treat, like they were going to eat giant gooey banana splits while watching cartoons. "Core strength is so important," she said. "It will help you with everything you do, from standing to running to swimming." She grinned around at the class.

"What about that stretching thing?" Charles

asked, forgetting to raise his hand. "Can't we do that first? It's good to warm up, right?"

Ms. Helm nodded and smiled. "Of course it is," she said. "That's why we'll start with jumping jacks. We'll do the stretches soon, I promise. I'm glad you're so eager to try them, Charles."

Charles groaned, but only inwardly, not out loud. Jumping jacks were definitely not on his list of favorite activities.

Once they were warmed up, Ms. Helm put them in groups and had them practice curl-ups, which Charles realized were basically the same as the sit-ups his dad did as part of his morning routine.

Charles was happy to be put together with Sammy and David. At least they were his friends, and they wouldn't laugh at him when he couldn't do a perfect curl-up. Sammy went first and did twenty-five in a row. His face turned pink, but he wasn't even breathing that hard. Charles went next. He did one curl-up, lay back on the mat, and groaned. This time, he didn't keep the groan inside. He groaned out loud.

Sammy and David giggled. "C'mon, dude, it's not that bad," said Sammy.

Charles tried another, lay back, and groaned even louder. This time Sammy and David laughed out loud. Charles grinned. Being laughed *at* was one thing. Making people laugh because you were doing something funny? That was a whole different thing. He started to groan and moan, louder and louder, and soon all the nearby groups were laughing, too.

"Charles."

He looked up to see Ms. Helm standing there, hands on hips. She was not wearing her usual smile. *Oops.*

"I'm glad to see that you are putting so much effort into your curl-ups," she said. "But I think your behavior is a little distracting. Take a time-out on the bleachers."

Charles gulped. He was in trouble again. At least Ms. Helm wasn't sending him to see the principal. He nodded and trudged off to take a seat. He perched on a hard wooden bleacher near one of the basketball hoops. He wished he could climb up to the top row, but he was pretty sure Ms. Helm would not like that. He put his elbows on his knees and his face in his hands, feeling like a ballplayer who had been sent to the bench.

Five minutes later, Ms. Guzman walked in.

Charles tried to look invisible, but after Ms. Guzman had a brief conversation with Ms. Helm, she walked over to sit next to him. She raised her eyebrows. "Not enjoying the curl-ups?" she asked. "I can't blame you. They don't look like fun to me, either." She clasped her hands around one of her knees and leaned back, peering at him. "But you know, Charles, sometimes we all have to do things that aren't so much fun. And we have to try to —"

"Do Our Best." Charles nodded. "Even when we don't want to. Like when I had to leave Nala this morning. I didn't want to, but I had to get to school on time."

"Nala?" Ms. Guzman asked.

"The stray dog. We caught her and brought her home!" Charles sat up straight and told Ms. Guzman the whole story. "Mom and Dad said we could foster her for a little while" — he hesitated and ducked his head — "but only if I stay out of trouble. If I mess up again, she's going to have to go somewhere else, like Caring Paws. She'll never get adopted from there. She's too shy. People like the dogs who come right up to them and act friendly."

He knew he was babbling a little, but Ms. Guzman just listened and nodded. Maybe it was good that he was distracting her. Maybe she wouldn't march him down to her office and call his parents. "Nala sounds like a lovely dog," she said. "And some people — me, for example — would rather have a shy dog than a mean or excitable one. I'm sure you'll find her a good home."

"I hope you're right. She's so sweet," Charles said. "Smart and cute, too. And she loves me."

"You're a lovable guy," said Ms. Guzman, tousling his hair. "Nala is lucky to have found you."

"I know, but I hated leaving her in the crate this morning. Mom had a meeting at work and Dad had to be at the firehouse." He explained that Nala had slept part of the night in the crate and hadn't seemed to mind it. (During the other part, she had been nestled up to him, under the covers.) "But still, I know she'll be bored and lonely without me," he said.

Ms. Guzman sighed. "I can relate. I feel the same way about leaving my dad home alone. He's been living with me for a while, ever since my mom passed away. Some days he goes to the senior center or takes a walk, but most of the time I think he's bored and lonely, too." She looked off into the distance, then seemed to come back to the bleachers. "I don't know why I'm telling you all that."

"Sorry about your mom," Charles said shyly.

Ms. Guzman smiled. "Thanks, Charles." She stood up and brushed off her skirt. "Nice talking to you. Take good care of that dog, okay?"

"I will," said Charles.

"And stick with this fitness thing. You might end up finding out that some of it is actually fun.

In any case, I hope I won't be hearing about you acting out again anytime soon."

"You won't," Charles promised. He watched her leave, hoping that their little chat had not counted as a real visit to the principal. He really had to watch himself and Do His Best. After all, Nala's future was at stake!

CHAPTER NINE

Charles headed straight home from school. "Sorry, I can't," he said when Sammy and David wanted to play soccer. "I'm grounded, remember?" He didn't really mind. He just wanted to be with Nala.

When he walked in the door, she scrambled into the hall with her tail waving and ears held high, nearly bowling him over in her excitement and happiness.

I missed you! It's been days and days, maybe a year! Where've you been?

Charles laughed as he kissed her soft head. He couldn't believe how far she had already come. Her coat gleamed after all the brushing he'd done; she was already fattening up a little; and best of all, she was losing some of her shyness. At least with Charles, Nala was really Doing Her Best.

"She still acts a little afraid of me," Mom said as she set out some apple slices and peanut butter for Charles's snack. "But she's warming up. She just needs to know she can trust a person."

"Any calls from the police or the shelters?" Charles asked.

"Not a word," Mom said. "I checked Facebook, too, in case anyone in the area was posting about a missing dog. I even took her down to the police station so they could check her with their microchip wand. Nothing. I guess she really is a stray."

Charles wanted to jump up, pump his fist, and shout, "Yeah!" but he didn't want to scare Nala. Instead, he just nodded. He was happy that they would get to foster the puppy a little longer — and hopefully find her the home she deserved.

He munched on his apple, wondering how much he needed to tell Mom about what had happened in gym class. Before he could even start, Lizzie burst in, with three friends in tow.

"Maria and Brianna and Daphne want to meet Nala," she said. "Ms. Dobbins says it's good for her to meet lots of people and get over her fear of strangers."

"Ooh, she's so cute!" said Daphne, rushing over to Nala, who lay near Charles's feet.

"Like a little Lassie!" said Maria. "Aww."

Nala shrank under Charles's chair.

"Hold on," said Charles, holding up his hands.

"Take it slow. One at a time, and keep your voices down." He sat down on the floor and took Nala into his arms. "It's okay, sweetie," he told her. "These people won't hurt you."

Nala let the girls pet her after she'd carefully sniffed the hands they held out, and she even licked Maria's cheek. Maria giggled. "Lizzie says this dog is crazy about you, Charles," she said.

Charles grinned. "I'm crazy about her, too," he said. It felt really good to know how much Nala liked him. Maybe, just maybe, Mom and Dad would let her stay, the way Buddy had stayed. Charles buried his face in Nala's fur, wishing he could keep her forever.

The next morning, the Peterson house was full of activity. Dad was heading to a training semi-nar, and Mom had an important interview lined up, so Charles and Lizzie got their own cereal and made themselves cheese sandwiches for lunch while their parents bustled around.

After breakfast, Charles took Nala up to his room. "You're going to have to stay in your crate for a little while," he said. "I'll be back right after school." Nala jumped onto his bed, turned around three times, and lay down. She thumped her tail as she glanced up at him with a doggy smile.

Can't I just stay right here? I promise to be good.

Charles knew he should put Nala in her crate, but so far she had not chewed up anything or had an accident in the house. She would be fine just hanging out in his room, wouldn't she? He grabbed his bookbag and kissed Nala good-bye, leaving the door open a little bit so Buddy could visit if he wanted. "Bye!" he yelled as he headed out the door.

He met Sammy and David at their usual corner. As they walked to school, his friends talked about the great scores they were getting in Fitness Club. "I'm going to do fifty curl-ups next time," Sammy boasted. "I bet no other second grader has ever done that many."

"I've been practicing my push-ups," David said. "Check out my muscles." He flexed a bicep like Popeye.

Charles still couldn't get excited about Fitness Club, even though he had promised Ms. Guzman he would Do His Best. He just kept thinking about Nala, hoping she wouldn't be too lonely while everybody was away.

They made it to school in plenty of time to join the usual game of kickball, then marched upstairs to room 2B when the bell rang. Mr. Mason smiled as he welcomed them into the classroom. "Good to see everybody here on time," he said. "We have lots to do today, so let's get settled quickly." Charles hung up his jacket in his cubby, then lugged his bookbag to his desk, opened it up, and pulled out workbooks and his pencil case.

They had all taken their places on the solar system rug in the corner, sitting "crisscross applesauce" for their morning meeting, when Mr. Mason looked up at the door and frowned. "Well, hello," he said. "What are you doing here?"

Charles followed his glance.

There was Nala, standing at the door.

As soon as she caught Charles's eye, her fluffy tail began to wag. She dashed across the room and leapt into his arms.

CHAPTER TEN

"Nala!" Charles buried his nose in her soft fur.

The puppy wriggled in his arms, whimpering with joy.

I found you! I found you!

Charles knew it was not good that Nala had escaped from the house. She must have slipped out when Mom or Dad or Lizzie had left, then trotted all by herself down the streets, and walked into the school and into his classroom. He should have been mad at her; he should have been telling her she was a naughty dog. But his heart swelled up and he felt tears come to his eyes. She loved him, this little dog. She really did. She had followed his trail all the way here. He shook his head and blinked back the tears as all the other kids in class jumped up to cluster around him.

"She's shy," he said. "Take it easy. One at a time."

Mr. Mason cleared his throat. When Charles looked up, he was smiling and shaking his head. "You and these dogs, Charles." He folded his arms and just watched for a little while, allowing the moment to happen. "Okay," he said when they had all cooed over Nala and let her sniff their hands and petted her gently. "As much as we'd all like Nala to be our classroom mascot today, we're going to have to let her go. We've got lots to do."

"Should I take her home?" Charles asked.

Mr. Mason shook his head. "I'd like you to take her down to the office. I know Mrs. Serota is fond of dogs; maybe she can watch Nala until one of your parents can come pick her up." He rummaged in his desk drawer and pulled out a long piece of string. "This will have to do for a leash."

Charles tied the string to Nala's collar and walked down to the principal's office. It felt strange to be walking a dog through the halls at school — like something in a dream. Nala didn't seem to think it was strange at all. She pranced along, holding her fluffy tail high. She grinned up at Charles.

It's great to be together, isn't it?

"Don't tell me," someone said. "This must be the famous Nala."

Charles looked up to see Ms. Guzman standing just outside her office, holding a clipboard. He gulped. "Um," he began. "She followed me . . . I mean, I didn't mean to —"

"Bring a dog to school?" Ms. Guzman raised her eyebrows. "Of course you didn't. But she's here now, isn't she?" She waved them into her office, and Charles sat down with Nala next to him. He explained that his parents were both busy for the rest of the morning.

"Mr. Mason said maybe Mrs. Serota could watch her," he finished.

Ms. Guzman got up and walked around her desk to hold out a hand to Nala, then scratched her gently between the ears. Nala sat very still, making Charles proud. She really was getting over her shyness.

"I'll watch her," said the principal.

Charles stared at her. "Really?"

"Sure," said Ms. Guzman. "She seems like a lovely pup. Has she been much trouble?" Now she was stroking Nala's soft white ruff.

"Not at all," said Charles. "She's great. Once she gets to know you, all she wants to do is be near you."

Ms. Guzman smiled and nodded. "Which is why she's here right now," she pointed out. "Isn't that right, little one?" she asked Nala. "You just wanted to be with Charles."

Nala wagged her tail and sniffed Ms. Guzman's hand.

You're a nice person, I can tell. I don't have to be afraid of you.

"Go," said Ms. Guzman, waving a hand at Charles. "I'll call your parents and I'm sure they'll show up as soon as they can. Meanwhile, this gal will be safe with me." She checked her watch. "Guess where you're supposed to be?" she asked.

Charles rolled his eyes. "PE," he said.

Ms. Guzman pointed to her poster. "Go," she said again. "And remember —"

"Do My Best," Charles said. "I know. I will."

Charles gave Nala a few pats, then headed for the gym. This was turning out to be a very strange day. As he pushed through the gym doors, he saw everyone in his class down on the mats, practicing the sit-and-reach stretch. *Yes!* he thought. This was the one event he felt good about. He and Lizzie had been stretching in the evenings as they sat watching the puppies play in the living room. By now, he could reach his fingertips past his toes. He found a spot near David and Sammy.

"Did you see Ms. Guzman? Was she mean?" David asked.

Sammy made the grizzly bear face, holding up his hands like claws. "Did she roar at you?" he asked.

Charles laughed. "Nope," he said. "In fact, she's taking care of Nala." He bent over and reached his fingers out over his legs, enjoying the good feeling of his muscles stretching.

"Nice work, Charles," said Ms. Helm, stopping by with a measuring tape. "You're very limber."

Charles smiled. "I'm doing my best," he said.

Through the rest of his morning classes, Charles could not stop thinking of Nala. He wondered if she had found a comfy place to lie down in Ms. Guzman's office, and he hoped that Ms. Guzman had remembered to give her a bowl of water. What if she needed to go outside? Would

Ms. Guzman recognize the signs and have time to take her? Finally, just as they were finishing up math class, the phone rang in room 2B.

"You're wanted in Ms. Guzman's office," Mr. Mason told Charles after he hung up.

Charles walked down to the office, working hard to resist the urge to break into a run. "Go on in," Mrs. Serota told him as he passed her desk. "They're all in there."

All? Charles wondered about that, but only for a moment. When he opened the door, he saw Ms. Guzman and both his parents and an older, bald man. The man was sitting in Ms. Guzman's chair, and in his lap sat Nala. He petted her ruff with long, bony fingers.

"Charles," said Ms. Guzman, "meet my father, Mr. Guzman. Dad, this is Charles, the boy I told you about. The one who's so good with dogs."

The old man held out his hand, and Charles shook it. "Um, looks like you're pretty good with dogs, too," he said to the man.

Mr. Guzman laughed. "Well, this one sure seems to like me," he said. "My daughter called me up and asked me to come down here to help her with something. I never expected that 'something' to be a pretty little pup like this."

"Nala took to Dad right away," said Ms. Guzman. "And I think he took to her, too."

Charles could see that the puppy was very comfortable in the old man's lap. He felt a twinge of jealousy. He was the one Nala loved, wasn't he?

"Charles," said Mom.

Her voice reminded Charles that he might be in trouble. And if he was in trouble, Nala was in trouble, too. Maybe this time, the little pup would really be headed for the shelter. "I can explain," he said. "I didn't put her in the crate this morning because —"

Mom shook her head, smiling. "It's okay," she said. "That wasn't the smartest thing to do, but in a way everything has worked out perfectly."

"What do you mean?" Charles asked.

Mom nodded toward Mr. Guzman. He was beaming. "My daughter and I would like to adopt this puppy, if that's all right with you," he said. "I think she'll make a perfect companion for me."

Ms. Guzman put a hand on her father's shoulder. "What do you think, Charles?" she asked.

For a moment, Charles was too surprised to say anything. Then he saw Nala reach her nose up to sniff Mr. Guzman's face. She wagged her tail as she licked the old man's cheek.

Charles knew that his parents were not likely to let him keep Nala. He reminded himself that fostering puppies meant giving them up when the right home came along — and it was obvious that Nala felt at home with Mr. Guzman. It was time to Do His Best for Nala. He took a deep breath. "I think that's a great idea," he said.

PUPPY TIPS

What should you do if you see a stray dog? The first thing is to tell an adult and ask for help. Don't chase the dog or try to catch her yourself. A dog that has been living on her own for a long time may be very frightened of people, and could even be dangerous. There may be a dog warden in your area, or workers at a local Humane Society who can help. Once the dog is caught, it's important to make sure she does not have an owner who is looking for a beloved pet. The best way to do that is to check with the local police and animal shelters, and have the dog scanned for a microchip. If the dog is truly a stray, then it's time to help find her a new forever home!

Dear Reader,

The first dogs I ever fostered were two young puppies who wandered into my yard and began to destroy my garden! They were adorable, so I forgave them. I checked around to find out if they had a home, and sure enough, they had been born at a nearby house. It turned out that the people there did not want the puppies, and when I offered to find them homes they were happy to let me do it. I found each puppy a wonderful forever home, and was able to see them and hear about them as they grew up into happy dogs. You can see a picture of the puppies on my website (www.ellenmiles.net), on the lower right side of the "About" page.

Yours from the Puppy Place,
Ellen Miles

P.S. For more stories about stray dogs, read LUCKY or NOODLE.

ABOUT THE AUTHOR

Ellen Miles loves dogs, which is why she has a great time writing the Puppy Place books. And guess what? She loves cats, too! (In fact, her very first pet was a beautiful tortoiseshell cat named Jenny.) That's why she came up with the Kitty Corner series. Ellen lives in Vermont and loves to be outdoors with her dog, Zipper, every day, walking, biking, skiing, or swimming, depending on the season. She also loves to read, cook, explore her beautiful state, play with dogs, and hang out with friends and family.

Visit Ellen at www.ellenmiles.net.